For my friend Anita and my granddaughter Elena,
both of whom have given me valuable
assistance in creating this book.
—MD

Mini picture book edition 2012
Copyright © 2009 by NordSüd Verlag AG, CH-8050 Zürich, Switzerland.
First published in Switzerland under the title *Heidi*.
English translation copyright © 2012 by NorthSouth Books Inc., New York 10016.
All rights reserved.

First published in the United States, Great Britain, Canada, Australia, and
New Zealand in 2012 by NorthSouth Books Inc., an imprint of NordSüd Verlag AG,
CH-8050 Zürich, Switzerland.

Translated by David Henry Wilson
Printed by Livonia Print, Riga, Latvia
ISBN: 978-3-314-10366-7
5th edition 2019

www.nord-sued.com

FSC
www.fsc.org
MIX
Paper from
responsible sources
FSC® C002795

Heidi

Johanna Spyri · Maja Dusíková

Adapted by Katja Alves

Nord Süd

From the friendly village of Maienfeld, a footpath leads through fields and forests up into the mountains.

One sunny June morning, a young woman climbed briskly up the steep Alpine path. Happily holding her hand was a little girl whose name was Heidi.

Heidi had lived with her Aunt Dete ever since she could remember. But now Dete had been offered a good job in Frankfurt, and Heidi could not go with her. So Dete was taking the little girl to live with her grandfather high on the mountain.

"Poor child! How can you possibly do such a thing?" said the people in the village below.

That was because everyone was afraid of the bad-tempered old man who lived all alone.

Grandfather was not happy to see them. "What will the child do here?" he growled.

When Dete left, Grandfather sat on his bench and smoked his pipe. He introduced Heidi to his two goats—one called Schwänli (Little Swan) and the other called Bärli (Little Bear). Then he gave Heidi some warm goat's milk.

"Do you like it?" asked Grandfather.

"It's the nicest milk I've ever had," said Heidi.

That night, Heidi slept in the hayloft on a bed of sweet-scented hay. Up in the loft was a round hole, and through the hole she could see far down into the valley below.

"It's lovely here," said Heidi happily.

The next morning, Heidi was awakened by a loud whistle. Outside was a boy and six goats. It was Peter, the goatherd. Grandfather brought Schwänli and Bärli out of their pen. "Would you like to go to the fields with them?" he asked Heidi.

"Oh, yes!" cried Heidi, who could think of nothing nicer.

Up on the mountain, Heidi ran through the wildflowers, leaping over rocks as she went. She laughed to watch the goats, who were even better jumpers.

Day after day, Heidi and Peter climbed the mountain to the high meadow. Heidi was as happy as the birds.

The summer soon passed, and it grew cold. One night, a deep snow fell. After this, the goatherd Peter did not come anymore.

Some mornings Grandfather fetched a sled, bundled up Heidi cozily, and off they flew, down the mountainside to Peter's hut. Peter's grandmother was waiting for them. She was blind and so she couldn't see how beautiful the mountains were. But Heidi described them to her and told her all about what she'd seen and done in the Alps. From then on, Peter's grandmother could hardly wait for Heidi to come again.

On their next visit, Grandfather mended the broken shutters, which banged against the wall of the house at night. "He has changed," thought the grandmother, "since Heidi came."

A whole year passed, and it was spring again. Aunt Dete came to visit them in the Alps. She had met a rich family in Frankfurt named the Sesemanns. Dete wanted to take Heidi back to Frankfurt with her so Heidi could learn how to read.

Grandfather was furious. He didn't want his granddaughter to turn into a stuck-up city girl. But, most of all, he could no longer imagine the mountain without her.

"If I go to Frankfurt, will I be able to come home in the evening?" asked Heidi.

"You can come home at any time," answered Dete. "And think of the lovely, soft white rolls you can bring the grandmother from Frankfurt."

This idea pleased Heidi, for she knew that Peter's grandmother could no longer chew that hard mountain bread.

And so Heidi left the mountain with Aunt Dete.

In Frankfurt Heidi made friends with Klara, the Sesemanns' daughter. The girl couldn't walk, and so she had to spend the whole day sitting in a wheelchair.

When Herr Sesemann went away on business, the very strict Fräulein Rottenmeier looked after the children. She had no sense of humor, and she always called Heidi by her full name: Adelheid.

Fortunately, the servant, Sebastian, was very nice. He gave them soft white rolls to eat with their soup. Heidi quickly hid hers so that she could keep them for Peter's grandmother.

When Heidi woke up in the morning, everything seemed very strange. From her bedroom window she could see nothing but gray walls and windows, and in the distance a tall church tower. Heidi longed for the rustle of the pine trees.

So one day, Heidi set off to find the church. Maybe from up in the tower she would be able to see the mountains!

Together with the warden of the tower, she climbed right to the top. But Heidi couldn't see any mountains. There was only a sea of roofs.

But something else in the tower made Heidi glad that she had come. The warden had a cat, and the cat had kittens.

"Oh, Klara would love these kittens so!" Heidi exclaimed, and the warden was happy to give her some of them.

"What's this? Cats?" shrieked Fräulein Rottenmeier in horror when Heidi came home. "Get rid of those horrible creatures!"

Luckily for Heidi and Klara, Sebastian liked cats and was happy to hide the kittens in the attic.

But Heidi could not stay out of trouble. A few days later, Fräulein Rottenmeier discovered all the rolls Heidi had been saving for the grandmother. "Throw this stale bread away!" she ordered.

"No! No!" begged Heidi. "Those rolls are for the grandmother!" And she burst into tears.

"Please don't cry so," said Klara. "I promise I will give you just as many rolls for the grandmother, or even more, when you go home."

One day, Klara's grandmamma came to visit. She brought with her a book full of wonderful pictures for Heidi to read.

"But I can't read," Heidi whispered.

Grandmamma took Heidi's hand. "You can learn to read," she said. "I will teach you. And when you learn, you may have this book to keep."

As the days passed, Grandmamma read stories from the beautiful book. Heidi often turned the pages and watched as Grandmamma showed her the words. By the time Grandmamma left, Heidi herself could read the stories to Klara.

Once more the autumn and winter passed, and it was spring again. Day after day, the girls read and played together; but Heidi missed her grandfather and Peter and the grandmother. She longed to be back in the mountains.

Then suddenly, strange things started happening in the Sesemann household. Every morning, the front door stood wide-open even though it was securely locked the night before.

"It's a ghost!" Fräulein Rottenmeier was certain of it.

Herr Sesemann came home at once. He did not believe in ghosts, but something was going on. Determined to find out what it was, he invited his friend the doctor to keep watch with him.

At the stroke of midnight, the men heard strange noises and jumped out from their hiding place. Standing in the doorway was a mysterious figure dressed in white.

It was Heidi!

The doctor and Herr Sesemann knew just what has wrong with Heidi. She was homesick! Heidi must be allowed to return to her home in the mountains.

Klara was very upset at the news, but her father promised to take Klara to visit Heidi in Switzerland that summer.

Heidi made the long journey holding in her lap a basket packed by Klara herself. It was full of soft white rolls for the grandmother.

"Grandfather! Grandfather!" she cried, beside herself with joy; and Grandfather, too, was happy to have Heidi back. At last she could sleep at night again. The pine trees rustled, and she knew that now she was home in the Alps once more.

As promised, Klara came in June. She loved the little house and the goats. She loved her days with Heidi and Grandfather. Heidi was delighted.

But Peter was jealous. Heidi was spending all her time with Klara. One day when they were all in the high meadow, he angrily pushed the wheelchair over a cliff.

Now Klara had to learn to walk on her own two feet, but Heidi helped her. Every day she improved . . . little by little . . . and before long Klara was completely cured.